For my spectacular agent,
Anne Clark – L.R.

For Olive Molly Mantle – B.M.

First published 2019 by Macmillan Children's Books
an imprint of Pan Macmillan
20 New Wharf Road, London N1 9RR
Associated companies throughout the world
www.panmacmillan.com

ISBN 978-1-5098-4597-2 (HB)
ISBN 978-1-5098-4598-9 (PB)

1 3 5 7 9 8 6 4 2

A CIP catalogue record for this book
is available from the British Library.

Printed in China

BEWARE
THE
CROC

Written by
Lucy Rowland

Illustrated by
Ben Mantle

DRACULA SPECTACULAR

MACMILLAN CHILDREN'S BOOKS

The Draculas lived in a house in the park.
It was creaky and crooked and dusty and dark,
With midnight-black ceilings, an inky-black floor,
Raven-black curtains and a batwing-black door.
Each day Mr Dracula said to his wife,
"How dreary! How dreadful! A wonderful life!"

Then later that year came a bundle of joy.
A Dracula baby arrived, "It's a boy!"

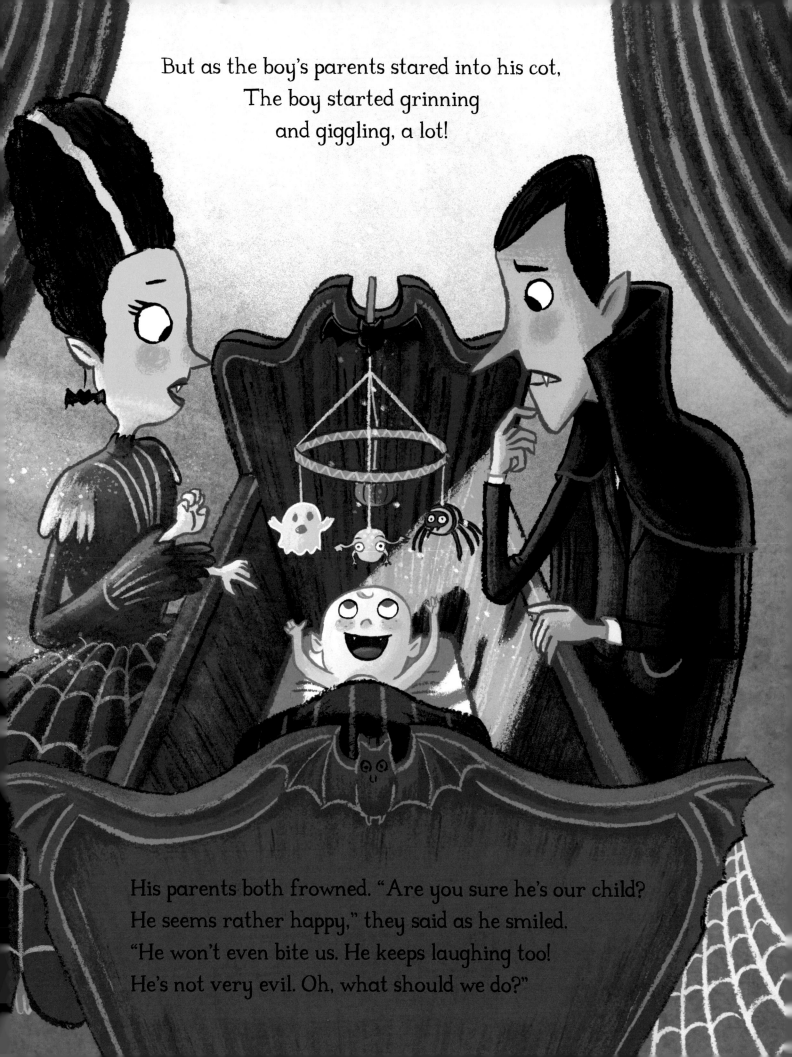

But as the boy's parents stared into his cot,
The boy started grinning
and giggling, a lot!

His parents both frowned. "Are you sure he's our child?
He seems rather happy," they said as he smiled.
"He won't even bite us. He keeps laughing too!
He's not very evil. Oh, what should we do?"

They both tried to teach
him to pounce and
to leap . . .

. . . To scare all his teddies,
to sneak and to creep.

S - SPOOKY
C - CHILLING
A - AAARGH
R - REALLYBAD
E - EERIE

But the Dracula child
just giggled with glee,
Then asked all his teddies
to join him for tea.

And what did he look like? He wouldn't wear black.
Not spider-black boots or a cloak on his back!
Then as he grew older, his dad warned, "At night,
You must stick to shadows. Don't go in light!"

When Dracula Boy flew alone through the street,
The children were frightened, "Don't bite us!" they'd shriek.

They jumped from their beds. They trembled and blubbered . . .

. . . And then stood and watched . . .

. . . as he browsed through their cupboard!

"They're lovely!" gasped
Dracula Boy with a titter.

He borrowed bright clothes
that were covered in glitter.

New clothes brought new friends. He was pleased as could be,
But the Dracula parents? They didn't agree!
They told him, "Now, Son, you must stop this tonight!
Go back to the town and give someone a fright!"

So wearing all black and a thunderous frown,
The Dracula boy headed back to the town.

He chose a small window and entered with dread,
Then heard some soft sobbing from under the bed.

"Who are *you*?" a girl sniffed, as she wrinkled her nose.
"This here is my room. See that sign? It says 'Rose'."
"I'm Dracula Boy and I'm sorry," he sighed.
"I don't want to scare you. I shouldn't have tried."

Rose huffed, "I'm not scared of a boy from the park,
I'm only afraid when it comes to the dark."

"But the dark," smiled Dracula Boy, "is so pretty!"
He gazed at the sparkling lights of the city.
"Just come and explore it. The dark doesn't hurt.
But first of all, please may I borrow that shirt?"

That night, they both giggled. They skipped and they walked.
They soared through the skies. They danced and they talked.

They noticed the fireflies twinkling bright
And the smatter of stars shining soft in the night.

"I'm tired," yawned Rose, "but this night has been fun!
Who knew that the moon could shine bright like the sun?"

"The sun?" whispered Dracula Boy in dismay,
"I'll never know colours as bright as the day."
Rose asked him, "Perhaps you could come back tomorrow?"
But Dracula Boy turned away, full of sorrow.

He thought of his dad and the earlier warning,
Then quickly flew home, just in time for the morning.

For nights he stayed in, he was quiet and sad.
"What's wrong with our son?" wondered Dracula Dad.

"Oh, how can we help him?" asked Dracula Mum.
"It makes me unhappy to see him so glum."

At last he went out and Mum searched for a clue
And Dracula Dad said, "I know what to do!"

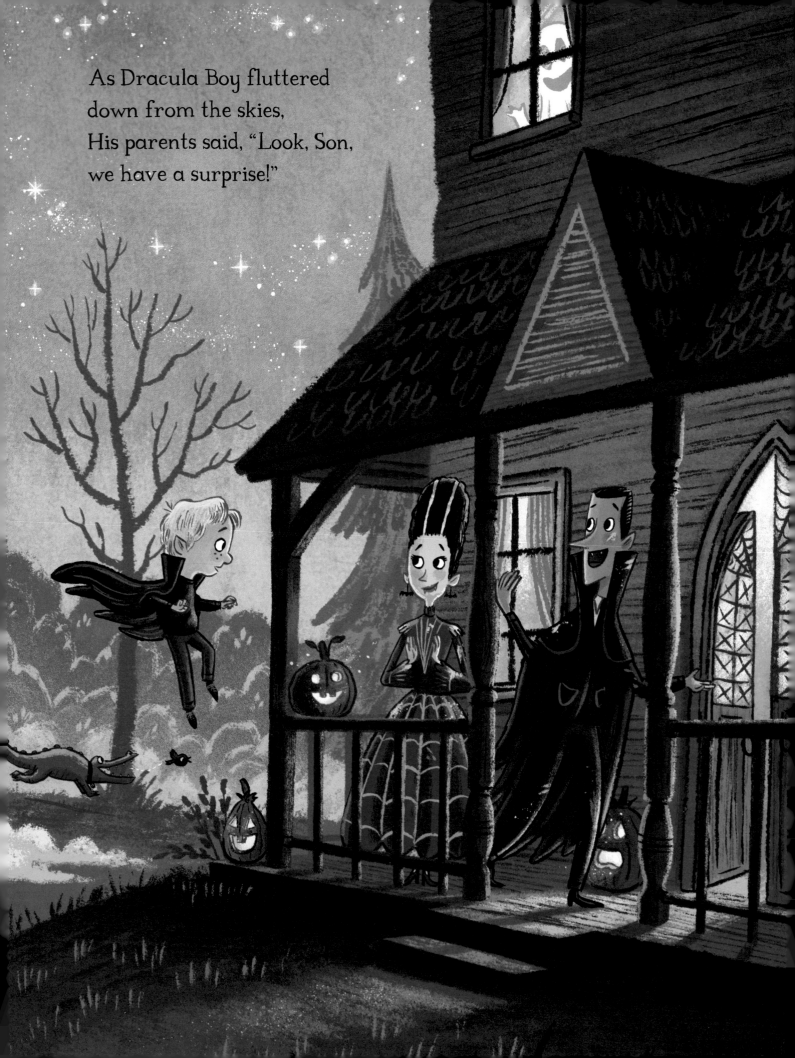

As Dracula Boy fluttered
down from the skies,
His parents said, "Look, Son,
we have a surprise!"

They'd painted the walls in his bedroom so bright,
With a big yellow sun and green trees and a kite.

His parents looked down at the daisy-specked floor
And grinned as they heard a small knock at the door.

The Draculas watched as Rose stepped through the smoke.
She gave her new friend a long rainbow-bright cloak
And giggled, "Hello! I've come round for the day.
Now, tell me, what games are we going to play?"

His parents beamed up at their colourful Dracula.
"Son," smiled Mum, "You look really spectacular!"
Dracula Dad said, "Now, go and have fun."
And Dracula Boy? Well, he glowed like the sun.